Hello, Reader!

Amanda wants to dance Clara in *The Nutcracker*.
So does her best friend, Emily.
Who will get the part?
And how will they stay best friends?

The girls from ALL TUTUS SHOULD BE PINK are back
in another story that will make you laugh!

Library of Congress Cataloging-in-Publication Data

Brownrigg, Sheri.
   Best friends wear pink tutus / by Sheri Brownrigg ; illustrated by Meredith Johnson.
       p.   cm. — (Hello reader)
   Summary: When two friends vie for a part in "The Nutcracker," who will get the part?
   ISBN 0-590-90738-7
   [1. Ballet dancing—Fiction. 2. Friendship—Fiction.] I. Johnson, Meredith, ill. II. Title. III. Series.
PZ7.B8243Be   1993
[E]—dc20
                                                                92-27569
                                                                    CIP
                                                                    AC

12 11 10 9   6 7 8/9

Printed in the U.S.A.   23

First Scholastic printing, September 1993

BEST FRIENDS Wear Pink Tutus

by Sheri Brownrigg
Illustrated by Meredith Johnson

SCHOLASTIC INC.

New York   Toronto   London   Auckland   Sydney

I'm Amanda,
and this is Emily.

We're best friends,
and we wear pink tutus.

We wear pink tutus to school.

We wear pink tutus to the store.

We even wear pink tutus
to go roller skating.

Best of all, we wear
our pink tutus to ballet class.

Our ballet class is going
to dance *The Nutcracker*.

Each student will try out for a part.
Our teacher, Miss Yvonne,
will decide who gets it.

I want to be Marie.
So does Emily.

Marie doesn't get to wear a pink tutu,
but she is the star of the show.

Miss Yvonne says
there can only be one Marie.

"I really want to be Marie," Emily says.
"But I really want to be Marie," I say.

If I get to be Marie, then Emily will be sad, and that will make me sad.

If Emily gets to be Marie, then I will be sad, and that will make Emily sad.

"Sometimes being your best friend is hard," Emily says.

For the tryouts, we decide not
to be best friends.

We warm up at opposite sides of the
room. We try not to look at each
other.

"Pretend you are Marie and show me how you would dance for your new Nutcracker doll," Miss Yvonne says.

Emily is dancing very well.
I think she may get the part.

Suddenly she sees me.

Emily acts dizzy and wobbles.

That's odd. Spinning never made
her dizzy before.

Now it's my turn. I point my toes
like a real ballerina.

Then I see Emily. I kick the doll over on purpose.

Oops! It's not time for the Nutcracker to lose his head yet!

Miss Yvonne picks Nicole to be Marie.
Nicole is an older girl.

"Amanda and Emily will be snowflakes in 'The Snowflake Waltz,'" says Miss Yvonne.

"Together?" I ask.

"Of course," says Miss Yvonne.

Miss Yvonne knows we dance better together.

And we know we dance better
when we are best friends.

Anyway, we would rather be snowflakes.
Snowflakes get to wear tutus.

I guess we are the first *pink* snowflakes
in the history of *The Nutcracker*!